I LOVE YOU, LITTLE MONKEY

For Kit with love—then, now and always
— A. D.

For Otilie and George, the other little monkeys!
—K. McE.

ISBN-13: 978-0-545-09436-8
ISBN-10: 0-545-09436-4

Text copyright © 2006 by Alan Durant. Illustrations copyright © 2006 by Katharine McEwen. All rights reserved. Published by Scholastic Inc., 557 Broadway, New York, NY 10012, by arrangement with Simon & Schuster Books for Young Readers, an imprint of Simon & Schuster Children's Publishing Division. SCHOLASTIC and associated logos are trademarks and/or registered trademarks of Scholastic Inc.

12 11 10 9   11 12 13/0

Printed in the U.S.A.   40

First Scholastic printing, May 2008

The text for this book is set in Hank.

The illustrations for this book are rendered in watercolor and colored pencil.

I LOVE YOU, LITTLE MONKEY

by Alan Durant

Illustrated by Katherine McEwen

SCHOLASTIC INC.
New York Toronto London Auckland Sydney
Mexico City New Delhi Hong Kong Buenos Aires

Deep in the jungle, beneath a great Big Tree, huffed one bored Little Monkey.

"Will you play with me?" he asked Big Monkey.

But Big Monkey was picking figs for supper and could not play.

"Little Monkey why don't you do some climbing?" asked Big Monkey.

So Little Monkey climbed.
He climbed up to the top
of the Big Tree . . .

and when he climbed down again,
he found Big Monkey's pile of figs.

He threw one at
the Big Tree.

SPLAT!

Little Monkey laughed.
He threw another fig . . .
and another and another.

SPLAT!
SPLAT!
SPLAT!

When Big Monkey came back,
there was only one fig left.

"That was naughty, Little Monkey,"
said Big Monkey. "Those figs were
for our supper! Now I'll have to go
and pick more."

"I'll help you,"
said Little Monkey.

So Little Monkey helped Big Monkey
pick figs for supper. Soon they were done.

"NOW will you play with me?"
asked Little Monkey.

"Not yet," said Big Monkey.
"First, I've got to make the beds.
Why don't you do some swinging
and jumping?"

So Little Monkey swung and
jumped in the Big Tree.

Then he saw the bed that
Big Monkey had made for him.

Little Monkey swung and
Little Monkey jumped.

WHEEE!

CRASH!

He landed right in the middle
of the bed and crushed it.

"Oh, that was naughty,
Little Monkey," said Big Monkey.
"Now I'll have to make your
bed all over again."

"I'll help you,"
said Little Monkey.

So Little Monkey helped
Big Monkey make his bed again.
Soon they were done.

"NOW will you play with me?"
asked Little Monkey.

"Not yet," said Big Monkey.
"First I need a little nap.
Why don't you play for a while?"
Big Monkey lay down
on his bed and . . .

Little Monkey played.

He danced . . .

and swung . . .

and jumped . . .

and . . .

WHOOPS!

. . . landed right on top of Big Monkey!

"You naughty monkey!"
shouted Big Monkey.
"Go up to your bed now!"

Little Monkey climbed
up to his bed.

He started to cry.

When Little Monkey came back down again,
Big Monkey put his arm around him.

"You don't love me,"
Little Monkey sobbed.

"Yes, I do,"
said Big Monkey.

"Do you love me when I'm naughty?"
asked Little Monkey.

"Of course I do," said Big Monkey.
"I may not like the naughty things you do,
but I love you always. Even when you're naughty.
Now, let's play swing-and-chase."

Little Monkey smiled.

Swing-and-chase was Little
Monkey's favorite game.

Big Monkey and Little Monkey
played and played . . . until at last
they came to a clearing around a large pool.

They stopped and had a drink.

Then Big Monkey took Little Monkey's
paw in his own.

"I'm sorry I did those naughty things."
said Little Monkey.

"And I'm sorry I shouted at you,"
said Big Monkey. "It was naughty of me
to shout at you."

Big Monkey gave Little Monkey
a great big hug.

"I love you, Little Monkey," he said.

Little Monkey climbed onto Big Monkey's back,
and they started for home.
"I love you, too, Big Monkey," whispered Little Monkey.

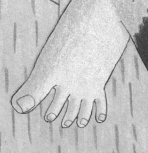

"I love you always. Even when *you're* naughty."